The Lost Kittens

Written by Karen Wallace
Illustrated by Jackie Harland

WAYLAND

The Lost Kittens

L

First published in 2010
by Wayland

Text copyright © Karen Wallace
Illustration copyright © Jackie Harland

Wayland
338 Euston Road
London NW1 3BH

Wayland Australia
Level 17/207 Kent Street
Sydney, NSW 2000

Series Editor: Louise John
Editor: Katie Powell
Cover design: Paul Cherrill
Design: D.R.ink
Consultant: Shirley Bickler

A CIP catalogue record for this book is available from the British Library.

ISBN 9780750263368

Printed in China

Wayland is a division of Hachette Children's Books,
an Hachette UK Company

www.hachette.co.uk

"I've lost my kittens," sobbed Cat. "What am I going to do?"

"Don't worry," said Dog. "I'm a detective. I'll find your kittens for you."

Dog looked all around the farmyard and inside the chicken house.

"Go away," said Hen, pecking Dog on the nose. "There are no kittens here."

Poor Dog! It wasn't easy being a detective.

Dog thought hard. There was something he needed to know.

"When did you last see your
kittens?" he asked Cat.

"Just a few minutes ago,"
said Cat. "They were asleep
on the hay so I went to get
something to eat."

"When I came back the
tractor had gone!" cried Cat.

Cow looked over the fence.
"That's because the farmer
drove it away," she mooed.

"Oh, no!" cried Cat. "I'll never see my kittens again!"

"Not so fast," said Dog.
He twitched his nose.
"If there's a trail, I'll find it!"

17

Dog looked down and spotted
some big tyre marks.

Dog sniffed the ground.
Kitten fur!

He set off to follow the trail.

Horse was standing in the
field eating grass.

"Have you seen a tractor?"
asked Dog.

Horse nodded and looked to
one side. "It went that way,"
he said.

Rabbit was munching on
a flower.

"Have you seen a tractor?"
asked Dog.

"Yes, I have," said Rabbit. She twitched her nose across the field. "It went that way."

Fox was half asleep in
the sun.
"Have you seen some kittens
on a tractor?" asked Dog.

"Why?" grinned Fox, with a
sly look on his face.

"Never mind," said Dog.
"I'll find them myself."

Dog followed the trail to
a big field, but all he found
was a pile of hay bales.
The tractor had gone!

Dog put his paws over
his head.

Suddenly, Dog heard a sound. Mew! Mew! He pricked up his ears and followed the sound.

It was the kittens! They had fallen off the bales onto the grass.

Dog carried the kittens back to the farm. Cat was delighted.

"Three cheers for Dog,"
she cried. "He's the best
detective ever!"

START READING is a series of highly enjoyable books for beginner readers. **The books have been carefully graded to match the Book Bands widely used in schools.** This enables readers to be sure they choose books that match their own reading ability.

Look out for the Band colour on the book in our Start Reading logo.

The Bands are:

Pink Band 1A & 1B

Red Band 2

Yellow Band 3

Blue Band 4

Green Band 5

Orange Band 6

Turquoise Band 7

Purple Band 8

Gold Band 9

START READING books can be read independently or shared with an adult. They promote the enjoyment of reading through satisfying stories supported by fun illustrations.

Karen Wallace was brought up in a log cabin in Canada. She has written lots of different books for children and even won a few awards. Karen likes writing funny books because she can laugh at her own jokes! She has two sons and two cats.

Jackie Harland is woken up every morning by her two cats taking it in turns to nibble her toes and pat her face with their paws. It works every time, and they always get their breakfast first. In spite of that, she loves them very much, and after she finally gets to eat her own breakfast, she loves painting, especially animals.